Retold by Annie North Bedford

Illustrated by Jean Chandler

A GOLDEN BOOK • NEW YORK

Western Publishing Company, Inc., Racine, Wisconsin 53404

TM & © 1992 Warner/Chappell Music, Inc. All rights reserved.
Printed in the U.S.A. No part of this book may be reproduced or copied
in any form without written permission from the publisher. FROSTY THE SNOWMAN,
the character likeness, and related indicia are trademarks of Warner/Chappell Music, Inc.
All other trademarks are the property of Western Publishing Company, Inc.
Library of Congress Catalog Card Number: 91-77936
ISBN: 0-307-00148-2   MCMXCII

ABOUT FROSTY

Frosty the Snowman was born in 1950 as the subject of a record album. He soon became enormously popular with children and adults alike. He stars in his own television special and has made numerous appearances in Thanksgiving and Christmas parades. Unlike other snow people, Frosty is at home even in the warmest parts of the world.

Frosty the Snowman came to town one bright, cold winter day.

The first real snow of the winter had fallen the night before. In the morning, out came the children, and they started to roll snowballs. Round and round the snowy yard they rolled the snowballs. Soon they had two fine big ones.

Round and round the yard again—there was a smaller snowball, just the right size for a snowman's head.

Billy and Sally found a broom and propped it up against the snowman.

Tommy ran home and brought back an old scarf for the snowman to wear around his neck.
Joe found two big buttons for the front of the snowman.

"Now we need a hat,"
said Sally.

So all the children went off
to see what they could find.

Sally found an old cap, but
it didn't look just right.

Billy found a battered felt hat,
but it still didn't seem right.

Just then, down the street came the whistling
wind. It blew a shiny top hat to their feet.
"Just what we need!" cried Sally.
"It's like magic!" said Tommy.

Tommy picked up the shiny top hat and put it on the snowman's head.

ZING! Tommy's hand sprang back with a shock.

"It *is* magic!" he gasped.

"So it is," said a deep, chuckly voice the children had never heard before. "And a pleasant sort of magic, if I do say so myself."

"It's the snowman!" whispered Sally.
And so it was.
"Frosty the Snowman, at your service," he said.
And that was how Frosty the Snowman
came to life.

If you've never had a snowman for a friend,
you can't begin to imagine all the fun those
children had.

Frosty took them sledding—and never had
their sleds gone so swiftly and so far.

Frosty helped them build a snow
house—and never had the blocks
packed so firmly and so well.

Then Frosty and the children all went ice-skating. The magical part was that while they were with Frosty, the children could stay out and play in the snow and never get shivery cold.

Was it Frosty's warm heart or his magical smile? Whatever it was, the children thought it was fine.

Each morning when the children came out to play, Frosty had a wonderful plan all set.

One morning he said, "Let's go shopping today. I've never seen a store, you know."

So they all joined hands and away they skipped, off toward town.

It was fun showing Frosty around.
He thought every window was wonderful,
especially the toy store.

All around town the children led
Frosty that day, while the warm,
wintry sun shone down.

Soon they came to a corner, and around
the corner came a warm, gusty wind. Off went
Frosty's hat, and away went Frosty after it.

Then *Tweet!* sang the traffic cop's loud whistle.
The children could not follow Frosty because
traffic was streaming by— buses and trucks
and cars.

Tweet! went the traffic cop's whistle again. The crossing stood empty, but there was no sign of Frosty.

Only his top hat rolled down the street,
all by itself in the melting snow.

"Officer!" Sally cried. "Where has
Frosty the Snowman gone?"

"Oh," said the police officer.
"Frosty the Snowman has gone away
 Where all snowmen go on a sunny day.
 But he'll be back at your bidding and call
 Whenever great heaps of snowflakes fall."

And he will!